SING A SONG OF SIXPENCE

BARRON'S

First edition for the United States
published 1988 by Barron's
Educational Series, Inc.

First published 1987 by
Hutchinson Children's Books
An imprint of Century Hutchinson Ltd
London, England

All inquiries should be addressed to:
Barron's Educational Series, Inc.
250 Wireless Boulevard
Hauppauge, New York 11788

Library of Congress Catalog Card No. 87–18829
International Standard Book No. 0–8120–5900–X

Printed in Italy

789 9680 987654321

SING A SONG OF SIXPENCE

ILLUSTRATED BY
RANDOLPH CALDECOTT

SERIES EDITOR · ELIZABETH RUDD

BARRON'S

NEW YORK

Sing a song of sixpence,
A pocket full of rye;

Four-and-twenty blackbirds,
Baked in a pie.

When the pie was opened,
The birds began to sing.

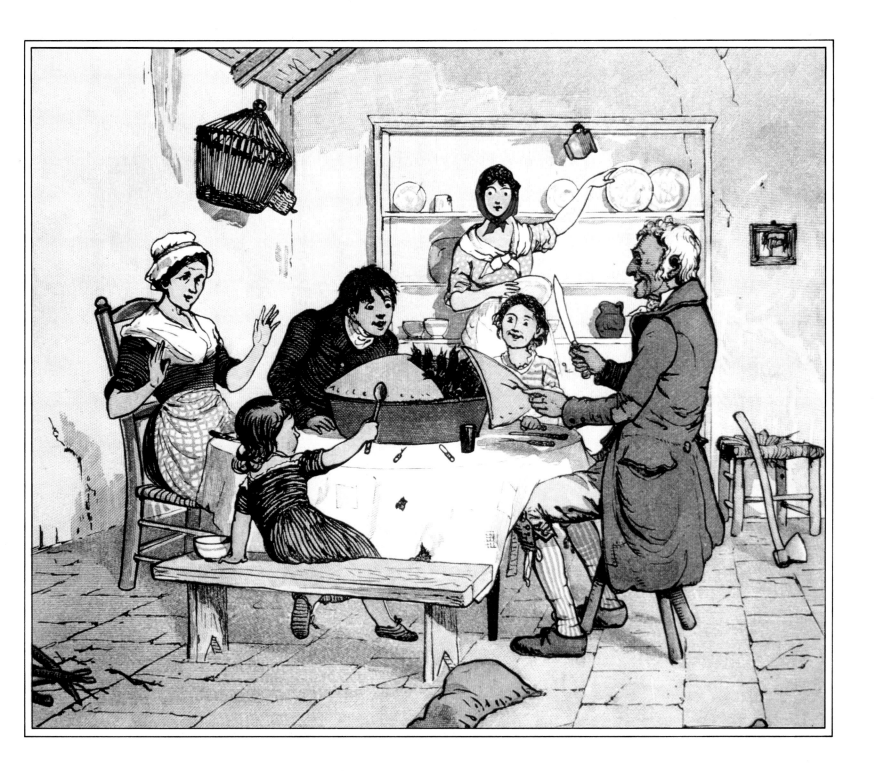

W asn't that a dainty dish,
To set before the king?

The king was in his counting house,
Counting out his money;

The queen was in the parlor,
Eating bread and honey;

The maid was in the garden
Hanging out the clothes,

W hen down came a blackbird
And snipped off her nose.

But then there came a little wren
And popped it on again.